Jean · Van · Leeuwen
Nothing Here But Trees
Pictures by Phil · Boatwright

Dial Books for Young Readers New York

To Ben and Annabella

P. B.
_____

Published by Dial Books for Young Readers
A member of Penguin Putnam Inc.
375 Hudson Street
New York, New York 10014

Text copyright © 1998 by Jean Van Leeuwen
Pictures copyright © 1998 by Phil Boatwright

Designed by Nancy R. Leo
Printed in Hong Kong
First Edition
1 3 5 7 9 10 8 6 4 2

Library of Congress Cataloging in Publication Data
Van Leeuwen, Jean.
Nothing here but trees / Jean Van Leeuwen; pictures by Phil Boatwright.—1st ed.
p.   cm.
Summary: A close-knit pioneer family carves out a new home amidst
the densely forested land of Ohio in the early nineteenth century.
ISBN 0-8037-2178-1 (trade).—ISBN 0-8037-2180-3 (library)
[1. Frontier and pioneer life—Ohio—Fiction. 2. Ohio—Fiction.]
I. Boatwright, Phil, ill. II. Title.
PZ7.V3273No 1998   [E]—dc21   97-34318   CIP   AC

*The art for this book was created using oil and acrylics. It was then
color-separated and reproduced as red, blue, yellow, and black halftones.*

In the early nineteenth century the middle part of the United States was unsettled wilderness. Stretching from the Pennsylvania border west to the Mississippi River, from the Ohio River north to the Great Lakes, the region was known as the Old Northwest. It was not until after the War of 1812 that settlers in large numbers began to push west into this new territory. They came because of hard economic times, the feeling that the East was becoming too settled, and descriptions by travelers of a land that was an "earthly paradise."

These new settlers came by wagon on wilderness roads, by boat on the river, on horseback, or even on foot. But when they arrived, what they found was a vast forest. Nearly all the land was covered with huge ancient trees, draped with thick vines. The trees were so tall that their trunks rose sixty feet before the first branch. They were so wide around that a man could easily live inside a hollow one. And they stood so close together that it was hard to see the sky.

Against this great forest the settler had only one weapon: his axe.

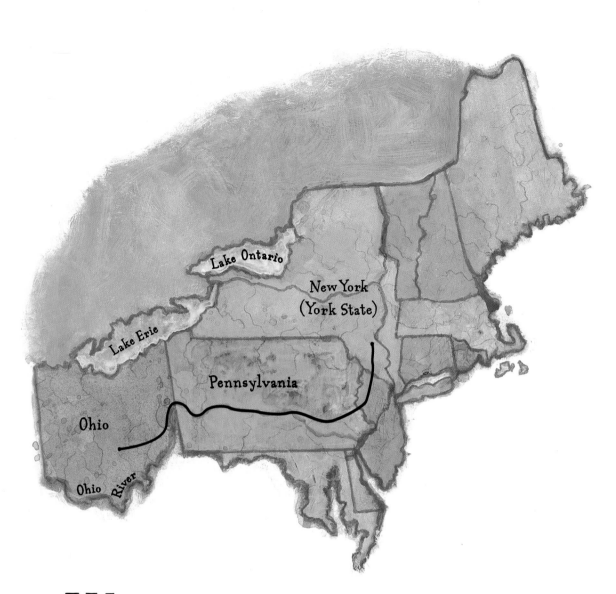

Lake Ontario

Lake Erie

New York
(York State)

Pennsylvania

Ohio

Ohio River

W E'D COME ALL THE WAY FROM YORK STATE.

Me and Willy and Pa and Ma and the three little ones, and the yellow dog
that followed us since the second day. We'd come by wagon and flatboat
and our own sore feet to this spot, in the new state of Ohio, where Pa
said we would make our farm.

Here? Me and Willy looked at each other. Nothing was here but trees.
Trees so thick and tall I couldn't make out their tops. Trees so wide Willy
and me and Pa and Ma together could not reach around them. Trees that
put me in mind of some dark, long-legged beasts, blocking out the sun.

Back home we'd had open fields and bright sky. And Ma's folks on the next farm. But there had been hard times too. Snow and cold and crops that failed two years running. It was on account of the hard times we left.

Pa wasn't one for talking. He just reached for his axe. By nightfall he had put up a lean-to of sapling logs that would do us for a shelter.

Next day he started on a clearing. *Tock, tock!* his axe rang out in the quiet. *Tock, tock, tock, tock!* Then came a groaning like a creature hurt. A long whooshing. And a thud that shook the earth.

A tree lay dead, like a fallen giant, on the mossy floor.

I peered up, looking for the sky. But it wasn't till the third day, just at noon, that a thin ray of sun came slanting through that dark green roof. It glimmered gold in the leaves. I saw it touch the ground.

Pa did too. I saw him smile.

For days his axe rang out. Trees fell in a jumble. Now the sun came for chunks of each day, brightening the gloom.

But there was a whispering in the woods. Like the trees were talking, I thought. Startled, I turned around. Leaves were falling.

Nights grew colder. Me and Willy piled more logs on the fire outside our lean-to. Still the baby woke up crying.

"Winter's a-coming," said Ma. Her cheeks were pinched like they'd been ever since we left her folks behind.

Pa nodded. "Best we start a cabin."

He cut and trimmed the straightest logs. Me and Willy and Ma helped lift them into place. Higher rose the cabin each day. As high as little Abby. "High as me," said Eliza. "Higher than me!" said Willy. Then came the roof, a stick-and-mud chimney, a door. Last Pa chopped a little hole for a window. Across it he laid a greased newspaper Ma had carried all the way from home.

Oh, it was a fine sight when the sun peeped through, lighting up our cabin all mellow.

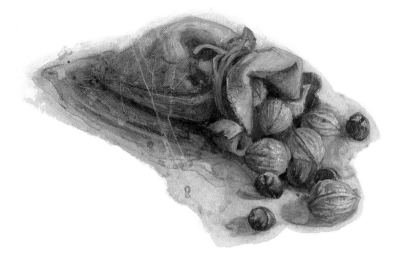

But more needed doing before winter came. Me and Willy and the little ones brought moss and sticks and clay from the river to chink the walls. Pa built a sleeping loft. Ma sent us to gather nuts.

Walnuts, we found, and hickory nuts too. One day I wandered off and happened on a butternut tree. I called out to Willy. No shout came back.

Sometimes he played tricks. "Willy!" I called again. Like as not he'd jump out at me. But no one answered. I looked for the sun, but the woods had gone dark. Which way was the cabin? All of a sudden every tree looked the same.

I tramped and tramped. Nothing did I see but trees. They hunched over me, shadowy dark, rustling like they were telling secrets. Or could those rustlings be some creature stalking me? Wolves. Or a panther.

Louder they grew. Closer. I picked up a branch for a club and turned to face whatever it might be.

"Scout!" I about bust out crying. It was our dog come to fetch me home.

Winter settled in. Pa went hunting and trapping. He brought home deer, and sometimes wild turkey. He set himself to furnishing the cabin, with beds, stools, an eating table. Ma sat spinning next to the fire.

"Now aren't we snug as a big old bear in its den," she said. And for the first time since we left home, she smiled.

Our meal sack was near empty. Still winter hung on. Snow was falling the day Pa set off with his skins for the trading post downriver. I watched him go till he was swallowed up by trees.

Dark set in, and Pa was not back. Ma said nothing, but brought the axe in next to the fire. That night, lying up in the loft with Willy, mice running across our feet, I heard wolves howling in the deep woods all around. It was a lonesome, fearsome sound.

Morning came, but not Pa. Afternoon. Looking out, it seemed like the trees had crept closer, hanging low, crowding us in. Ma was shaking out the last of the cornmeal for supper when Scout gave a joyful bark.

"Pa!" cried the little ones.

He brought a sack of meal, two fresh-killed rabbits, and best of all, salt.

Spring came. Pa took up his axe again. Trees fell, until he had near two acres cleared for planting. The stumps he left, but me and Willy grubbed out roots. We piled up logs and brush for a fence to keep out wild creatures.

It was a fine warm day when we heard it. A bird sound, I first thought. Or an Indian sound. But Pa had heard tell the Indians hereabouts had moved west. Faint it was, but steady. A dull *thunk, thunk.*

Three days, off and on, we heard it. Then Pa picked up his rifle.

"Can me and Willy come too?" I asked. Pa looked at us, then nodded.

We followed him, along the river, up a hill, down. Ahead I saw a brightening in the trees. Then I knew that sound. It was the *tock, tock* of an axe.

Crocker, the man's name was. He had a clearing bigger than ours and an ox to haul things and a cabin full of young ones. Me and Willy stared at them.

"Mighty glad to meet you," he told Pa.

We were no longer alone in these woods.

It was planting time. With his axe Pa gashed the ground and planted seed corn and potatoes. Ma marked off a little patch near the cabin. She sang as she dropped in the seeds she'd brought along: pumpkins, peppers, gourds, turnips. In a few weeks young plants were waving green all around the tree stumps.

But creatures came out of the woods to steal our crops. Deer and coons by night. Squirrels and birds by day. Willy made a drum from a hollow log. He and the little ones marched up and down the rows, scaring them off.

The days grew hot. The corn grew tall. Me and Willy hoed between the rows. I was hoeing late one day when the corn rippled behind me.

"Willy?" I said. Could be he was playing one of his jokes.

I turned around and looked at a bear. It was so close I could make out the little black eyes in its huge shaggy head. I stopped breathing.

The bear looked at me. I looked at the bear. Where was Pa?

"Don't move," he said softly. I saw he had his rifle ready.

A fly buzzed on the bear's nose. The bear swiped at it with one great paw. I leaned on the hoe to stop shaking. Then the bear turned and ambled back into the woods, mowing down corn as it went.

Some days when our hoeing was done, me and Willy went down to the river. It was cool and full of fish. Ma said a fish dinner made a change from all that game. I sat still, dangling my line and my feet. But Willy jumped on rocks and balanced on logs till he fell in, scaring the fish.

He was the one first heard the buzzing. "Bees!" he said.

Dropping our lines, we followed the sound. Through the trees, louder, till buzzing filled our ears. And we came on a hollow walnut tree.

"Wait till we tell Ma we found some sweetening!" said Willy.

That tree held honey, I knew. But Pa wouldn't chop it down till fall, when the bees had it chockful. So I took my knife and carved our initials. Now anyone passing would know this was our bee tree.

It was late summer. Harvesting time. Our clearing was a patch of gold against the dark, towering trees. We picked pumpkins, dug potatoes, cut corn. Pa said we had harvested more among the stumps than in the fields back in York State. If he could, he'd trade some corn for a milk cow.

"Come spring," he said, "we'll clear more land and plant wheat."

Leaves drifted down, splashing yellow and red. Me and Willy stacked
a woodpile near as high as the cabin. Ma holed up potatoes and turnips
for winter.

With Eliza and Abby helping, she hung strings of red pepper and pumpkin slices in the loft to dry. In hollow gourds she stored seeds for next spring's planting.

Then came the day Pa said, "Time to take down that bee tree."

Me and Willy carried all the buckets we had and Ma's big washtub. Pa started in chopping, then stopped.

"You boys want to take a turn?" he said.

It was the first time ever I got to swing Pa's axe. Mighty heavy it was. I scarcely made a mark. But I kept swinging like I always watched him do. At last chips began to fly. Then Willy had a turn, and Pa finished it off.

Pa smoked out the bees and spaded out the honey. We walked home, our buckets overflowing. Ma laughed when she saw them. And that night we had all the honey we wanted on our johnnycakes.

The trees were bare when Mr. Crocker brought his ox to help Pa clear our field. His wife and young ones came too. Three big boys and two little girls and a boy my size. "Name's Jeb," he said, looking at his feet.

Axes flew. The men cut up the black skeletons of trees lying all around. They pulled and pried the logs into piles. Me and Willy and Jeb helped. All day we worked, till I was fit to keel over. Then Ma called us to dinner.

Roast venison we ate, and rabbit stew. Potatoes, turnips, and johnny-cakes. And apple pie Mrs. Crocker had brought along. Me and Willy had three slices. We hadn't had pie since we left York State.

After dinner, while the older folks told stories, me and Willy and Jeb
wrestled and had races, and the little ones ran around with the dogs till
they all fell asleep in piles. It was near dark when the Crockers left.

"We'll come help with your barn raising," Ma said, smiling. She had
been smiling all day.

That night Pa set the logs to burning. Flames leaped and sparks flew.
The dark night blazed up with red. Watching from the doorway, I thought
I saw those great legs of trees take a step back.

Seemed like Pa was thinking the same.

"I believe we took a mite of them woods for our own," he said.

For days the fires smoldered, licking away at the great log heaps.
They filled the air with blue smoke, so thick I thought I'd always taste
it. They glowed red in the night. At last they burned out.

Snow fell, covering the ashes. Next morning I went out to the woodpile.

The trees were still there, standing near as tall and thick and fearsome as when Pa first swung his axe at them. But I saw spaces too. Trickles of paths. Sunlight shafting down here and there. The Crockers' clearing over yonder. Downriver, the trading post.

And our cabin, sending up a thin curl of smoke into blue sky.

E
VAN

2-3

$15.89

Van Leeuwen, Jean.

Nothing here but
trees.

39545000685502

DATE			

BAKER & TAYLOR